The Pobble
who has no toes

The Pobble who

Edward Lear

Illustrated by Kevin W. Maddison

A Studio Book
The Viking Press
New York

has no toes

Illustrations Copyright © Kevin W. Maddison 1977

Published in 1978 by The Viking Press
625 Madison Avenue, New York, N.Y. 10022

Published simultaneously in Canada by
Penguin Books Canada Limited

Produced by Ash & Grant Limited
120B Pentonville Road, London N1 9JB

Library of Congress Cataloging in Publication Data
Lear, Edward, 1812-1888.
    The pobble who has no toes (A Studio book)
    Summary: Reveals how the Pobble came to lose his toes and
    what happened afterward.
    [1. Nonsense verses] I. Maddison, Kevin W. II. Title.
PR4879. L2P6 1978 821′.8 77-24913
ISBN 0-670-56168-1

Printed in Great Britain

The Pobble who has no toes
Had once as many as we;
When they said, 'Some day you may lose them all;'–
He replied,–'Fish fiddle de-dee!'

And his Aunt Jobiska made him drink,
Lavender water tinged with pink,
For she said, 'The World in general knows
There's nothing so good for a Pobble's toes!'

The Pobble who has no toes,
Swam across the Bristol Channel;
But before he set out he wrapped his nose
In a piece of scarlet flannel.

For his Aunt Jobiska said, 'No harm
Can come to his toes if his nose is warm;
And it's perfectly known that a Pobble's toes
Are safe,—provided he minds his nose.'

The Pobble swam fast and well,
And when boats or ships came near him
He tinkledy-binkledy-winkled a bell,
So that all the world could hear him.

And all the Sailors and Admirals cried,
When they saw him nearing the further side,-
'He has gone to fish, for his Aunt Jobiska's
Runcible Cat with crimson whiskers!'

But before he touched the shore,
The shore of the Bristol Channel,
A sea-green Porpoise carried away
His wrapper of scarlet flannel.

And when he came to observe his feet,
Formerly garnished with toes so neat,
His face at once became forlorn
On perceiving that all his toes were gone!

And nobody ever knew
From that dark day to the present,
Whoso had taken the Pobble's toes,
In a manner so far from pleasant.

Whether the shrimps or crawfish gray,
Or crafty Mermaids stole them away—
Nobody knew; and nobody knows
How the Pobble was robbed of his twice five toes!

The Pobble who has no toes
Was placed in a friendly Bark,
And they rowed him back, and carried him up,
To his Aunt Jobiska's Park.

And she made him a feast at his earnest wish
Of eggs and buttercups fried with fish; –
And she said,–'It's a fact the whole world knows,
That Pobbles are happier without their toes.'